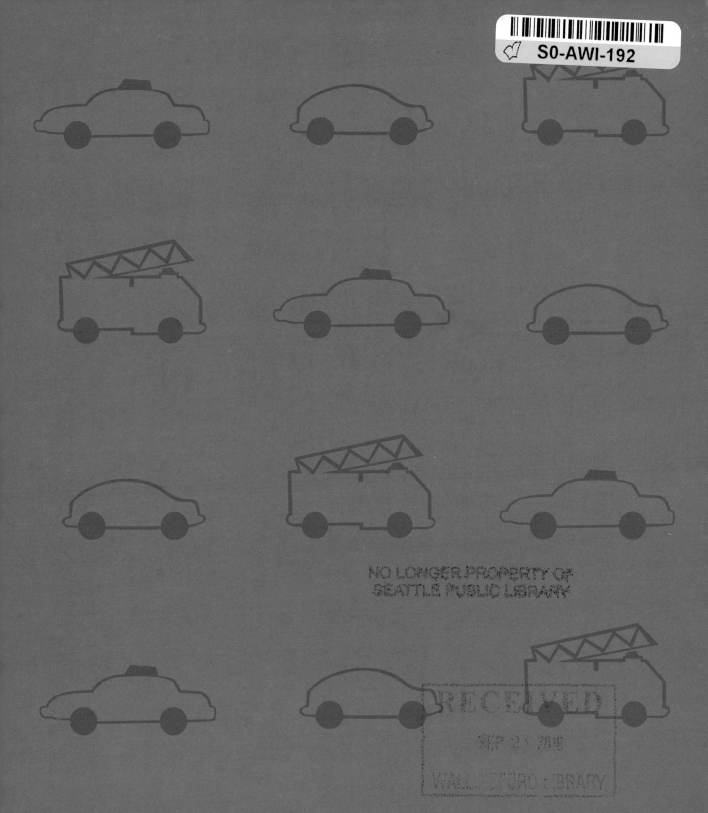

For my extended family and my city
—ST

For all my friends in New York City. I miss you!
—CL

Library of Congress Cataloging-in-Publication data is on file with the publisher.

Text copyright © 2019 by Sue Tarsky
Illustrations copyright © 2019 by Claire Lordon
First published in the United States of America in 2019 by Albert Whitman & Company
ISBN 978-0-8075-7728-8 (hardcover)
ISBN 978-0-8075-7722-6 (ebook)

Printed in China
10 9 8 7 6 5 4 3 2 1 WKT 24 23 22 21 20 19

Design by Rick DeMonico

For more information about Albert Whitman & Company,
visit our website at www.albertwhitman.com.

100 Years of Albert Whitman & Company
Celebrate with us in 2019!

Taking a Walk
Winter
in the
City

Sue Tarsky

illustrated by
Claire Lordon

Albert Whitman & Company
Chicago, Illinois

I went for a walk in the city today.
I saw lots of people rushing
in different directions.

I could only see their noses!

I went for a walk in the city today.

I saw lots of people rushing,

and one black cat drinking milk from a saucer.

The cat meowed at me!

I went for a walk in the city today.
I saw lots of people rushing,
one black cat drinking milk,
and two orange delivery trucks unloading boxes.

The delivery men waved to me!

I went for a walk in the city today.
I saw lots of people rushing,
one black cat drinking milk,
two orange delivery trucks unloading boxes,
and three red fire engines.

The fire trucks had their hoses out!

I went for a walk in the city today.

I saw lots of people rushing,

one black cat drinking milk,

two orange delivery trucks unloading boxes,

three red fire engines, and four flower and fruit stands.

The colors of the flowers and fruit looked like a rainbow!

I went for a walk in the city today.

I saw lots of people rushing,

one black cat drinking milk,

two orange delivery trucks unloading boxes,

three red fire engines, four flower and fruit stands,

and five striped awnings over a row of little shops.

Water was pouring down the awnings!

I went for a walk in the city today.

I saw lots of people rushing,

one black cat drinking milk,

two orange delivery trucks unloading boxes,

three red fire engines, four flower and fruit stands,

five striped awnings over a row of little shops,

and six dogs on leashes pulling in different directions.

The dogs all barked at me!

I went for a walk in the city today.

I saw lots of people rushing,

one black cat drinking milk, two orange delivery

trucks unloading boxes, three red fire engines,

four flower and fruit stands,

five striped awnings over a row of little shops,

six dogs on leashes pulling in different directions,

and seven broken umbrellas.

The umbrellas were blowing in the wind!

I went for a walk in the city today.
I saw lots of people rushing,
one black cat drinking milk,
two orange delivery trucks unloading boxes,
three red fire engines, four flower and fruit stands,
five striped awnings over a row of little shops,
six dogs on leashes pulling in different directions,
seven broken umbrellas,
and eight pairs of yellow rubber boots.

The boots were lined up outside a door!

I went for a walk in the city today.
I saw lots of people rushing,
one black cat drinking milk,
two orange delivery trucks unloading boxes,
three red fire engines, four flower and fruit stands,
five striped awnings over a row of little shops,
six dogs on leashes pulling in different directions,
seven broken umbrellas,
eight pairs of yellow rubber boots,
and nine blue cars whizzing past.

The cars all had their lights on!

I went for a walk in the city today.

I saw lots of people rushing,

one black cat drinking milk,

two orange delivery trucks unloading boxes,

three red fire engines, four flower and fruit stands,

five striped awnings over a row of little shops,

six dogs on leashes pulling in different directions,

seven broken umbrellas,

eight pairs of yellow rubber boots,

nine blue cars whizzing past, and ten gray pigeons.

The pigeons bobbed their heads and cooed at me!

I went for a walk in the city today. I saw

lots of people rushing

1 black cat drinking milk

2 orange delivery trucks
unloading boxes

3 three red fire engines

4 flower and fruit stands

5 striped awnings
over a row of little shops

6 dogs on leashes
pulling in different directions

7 broken umbrellas

8 pairs of yellow rubber boots

9 blue cars whizzing past

and 10 gray pigeons
bobbing their heads.

What a good walk I had!